Get lost, Lola

Also in the Totally Tom series:

1: Tell Me the Truth, Tom!

2: Watch Out, Wayne

4: Keep the Noise Down, Kingsley

5: Drop Dead, Danielle!

6: Don't Make Me Laugh, Liam

Get lost, Lola

Jenny Oldfield

Illustrated by
Neal Layton

Hodder
Children's
Books

a division of Hodder Headline Limited

One

Tom Bean grabbed his invitation, his cap and his board.

'What about your lunch?' his mum, Beth, yelled from the kitchen.

'No time!' Tom flew out of the front door.

'It's only one o'clock!'

'I know. I'm hooking up with Kingsley. We have to build the course for the jam!' Tom swivelled the peak of his cap round to the back and slapped his board on to the pavement.

'What jam? Do you need these?' Beth appeared at the door with a pair of sunglasses and a carrier bag full of stickers.

'Yeah!' Tom snatched the shades and put them on. Clutching the bag, he set off down the street. 'The skate jam!' he called over his shoulder. 'All the gnarly skaters are gonna be there!'

'Oh, yes, the gnarly skaters...' Beth echoed, shaking her head and smiling. 'You take care on that blessed board!'

But Tom was already way gone.

'And Tom Bean licks those slick tricks! He pulls that elusive move that non-pros drool over. Who can ever forget seeing Tom loop-the-loop round the massive circular pipe? Or pull the sickest air trick off a five-metre ramp, with a hundred camcorders capturing the cool moment? There may be a dozen other pros around trying to pull this stuff,

but they'll have a long way to go to match Tom Bean!'

Tom made up his own commentary as he skated along. Today was gonna be crucial, thanks to Kingsley's well cool idea.

'Hey, let's have a skateboarding party!' Kingsley had suggested, as he, Tom, Jimmy Black and Kalid were watching a skating vid at Kalid's house.

Tom had been concentrating on a slow-motion sequence showing a fakie tail stall, and had only come in on the discussion when plans had already been made.

'Sunday the 21st,' Jimmy had suggested. 'The Steelers are playing away that weekend, so there's no footie to watch.'

'In the park,' Kalid had added. 'We can build special ramps and verts, invite the whole crew, have a sticker toss, get our picture in the local paper...'

'What's going on?' Tom had cut in.

'Wash your lugs out!' Kingsley had bellowed, pouncing on Tom and dragging him away from the TV screen. 'We're gonna have a meet and hook up with other skaters. We'll put up a poster in the skate shop, do proper invites, the whole thing!'

'Rad plan!' Tom had agreed.

He'd done the poster for Slammer, the skateboard shop, using cut-out figures of American and Aussie kids—pulling super

stunts, whizzing, twirling and flying through
the air on their boards–from *Crusha*
magazine. Along the top of the poster he'd
printed the words, 'It's your party!' in Day-
Glo green, with all the info underneath.
Date, time, place–plus the fact that there
would be two contests: a street section
and a vert section, with prizes donated
by Slammer.

And now, on a bright windy day, it had
all come together. They were expecting
thirty skaters and a crowd of supporters,
the owner of Slammer, plus the bag full
of stickers, which Tom brought, and skate
goodies as prizes.

'Hey, Tom! Down here!' Kingsley's
yell brought Tom speeding downhill into
the park.

Tom pulled a Smithgrind along the kerb,
then tic-tacked across the flat tarmac area,
especially surfaced for skateboarders. He
saw that Kingsley's dad had already
unloaded the big, U-shaped ramp from the

back of his builder's truck. They were going to use the ramp for the vert section of the contest. Tom bailed quickly and ran to drag the ramp into place.

'Let me help,' a voice offered. Lola Kidman had raced along from the direction of the Riverside Café, dark hair streaming in the wind. She wore trainers, combats and a white sweatshirt, with the exact same style of shades as Tom.

'Grab this end,' Kingsley told her.

So Super-muscles Kidman heaved and shoved until they were satisfied with the ramp's position.

'Radical!' Kingsley gasped, standing up straight. He, too, was dressed skater cool in baggy black trousers and a death skull black T-shirt. He wore a baseball cap moulded to the shape of his head, with no sign of the short, curly black hair underneath.

Before long other kids began to arrive. Ryan showed up with a boy called Jared from another school, then Sasha and Danielle from Tom's own class.

'Oh, no! Look who's coming!' Tom groaned. Danielle was the type who always passed sneaky comments and dobbed you in if you'd done something wrong. 'What are they doing here?'

'They've come to support me,' Lola explained.

'Are you entering the competition?' Tom's jaw dropped. *Swimming* was Lola's thing, not skateboarding. Everyone knew that Lola was a complete beginner, a grommet.

'Sure,' she answered. 'I've been practising!'

'Yeah, well, you'll have to beat Kingsley,'

Tom grunted. *And me.* He wasn't sure he liked this unexpected rival. After all, Lola was a rad swimmer, tennis player and sprinter–without muscling in on the boarding, too!

'Hi, Lola!' Danielle and Sasha sang out. They perched on the edge of the vert, just where skaters wanted to run through their moves.

'Watch out!' New arrival Ryan plunged into the bottom of the ramp and shot out the other side. His trucks rumbled noisily over the hollow surface.

'Ooh!' Danielle and Sasha squealed and jumped clear.

'Spectators have to stay on the grass!' Kingsley warned, practising a high jump over a plank laid across two piles of bricks. He leaped over the wood while his deck went underneath, then he landed neatly back onboard.

'OK. Two o'clock, time to start!' Kingsley's dad, Wesley Harris, had stuck around, linked up with Dino Cole from Slammer to organise the sticker toss, and was now ready to start the contest.

Tom felt his stomach twist into knots. Sure, this contest was for fun only, no big deal. But doing OK was still important, and falling flat on your face in front of everyone would dent more than his head. It was his street cred that was at stake here.

'Nervous?' Lola whispered from her place behind him in the queue.

'No!' he said, high and sharp. For his street run he planned a 50-50, a tic-tac and a couple of pop shove-its, finishing with a Smithgrind into a wheelie. He went through them carefully in his mind.

Eight or ten kids went before him. Some zoomed round every centimetre of the course, covering the ground. Others went for one or two rad moves. Five had to bail.

'Time to strut your stuff, Tom!' Wesley called. He and Dino were the competition judges.

Tom took a deep breath. *You've done this a thousand times!* he reminded himself as he ollied on to the kerb. *Arms wide, keep your balance, let your knees take the shock...*

'...Wicked!' Lola whispered, as Tom returned to base.

He'd done it exactly according to plan!

Lola was pretty gnarly, too. She impressed the judges with a kickturn and 360, speeding along, flipping and flicking her board.

'Not bad for a grommet!' She grinned as she finished.

Tom saw that she had scored just two points less than him.

'Cool,' he grunted.

At the end of the first round, Kingsley was in the lead, with Ryan second, Tom third, and Lola fourth.

Now for the vert! Tom waited his turn, then dropped into the half-pipe to pull an axle stall at the far lip.

'Yeah!' The other contestants applauded

by slamming their boards down on the tarmac. Tom was well gnarly. He nailed a fakie tail stall and the deck bangers went crazy.

Another near-perfect run! He made a running stop and gave a big sigh of relief.

But Lola wasn't so lucky this time. Pulling a rock 'n' roll at the start of her routine, she leaned too far back and had to bail on to the tarmac. She landed hard on her bum, while her deck clattered into the crowd.

'Tough,' Tom murmured, picking up her dented board.

Lola snatched it from him. 'Get lost, Tom!'

'No, I mean it.'

'Whatever.' Lola glowered, ready to stomp away.

'Lola–are you OK?' Danielle ran up to make a fuss. 'Did you hurt yourself?'

'Leave me alone!' The only thing that was hurt was Lola's pride. Now she wanted to hide and forget the stupid contest.

'Yeah, leave her,' Tom echoed.

'Whoo-ooh!' Danielle and Sasha cooed.
'Listen to Tom Bean sticking up for Lola!'

'Get lost!' he told them.

'Tom Bean fancies Lola Kidman!' they
chorused.

'Shurrup! I don't! Get blinking lost!'
Turning his back, Tom listened to the final
result. Kingsley had slipped from first to
third, while Ryan and Tom had moved up to

first and second. That meant a complete new deck for Ryan and a new set of wheels for Tom, with Kingsley going up to receive a reel of grip-tape from Dino.

'And now are you ready for the sticker toss?' the shopkeeper asked.

Thirty pairs of hands reached for the customised stickers as Dino threw them in the air and scattered them. Tom grabbed a couple, then landed under a scrum of bodies.

'Cool!' he gasped to Kingsley as he emerged, his brown hair more messed up than usual, his cap half off his head. He grinned at the scene of scrummaging kids, then took a deep breath.

'Has this been a rad day, or what!'

Two

'Now don't breathe a word to your dad!'
Beth warned Tom and Nick the next
morning. Harry Bean was out delivering
mail as usual, while the rest of the family
ate breakfast.

'Are you listening?' Beth insisted,
switching off the telly.

'Aw, Mum!' Tom protested, through a
mouth full of cornflakes.

Nick scraped back his chair and grabbed his school bag. 'See ya!'

'Hold it! Listen, you two–I mean it! This birthday party is special. Your dad's fifty, and I'm planning a big surprise.'

'Yeah, yeah–got it, Mum.' Nick drifted out of the kitchen into the yard, where he unchained his bike and cycled off.

'It's you I'm really getting at, Tom.' Beth whipped the cornflake bowl from beneath her youngest son's nose. 'I know you and your big mouth!'

'Hey!' Tom attempted to scoop the last spoonful of milk and sugar from the vanishing bowl.

'Now–' Beth held the bowl out of reach,' –that I have I got your undivided attention...I'll tell you again. We are planning a big birthday bash for your dear old dad. This coming Saturday. Everyone will be here, we'll have a massive cake, balloons, music and a video compilation of all the big moments in our family life.

Got it?' Beth dropped Tom's cereal bowl into the sink.

'But there was still some left!' he wailed.

His mum picked up three videos and waved them at him. 'I want you to take these into school with you and give them to Lola Kidman.'

'Whaffer?' Tom tried to cram one piece of toast into his mouth before Beth snatched it out again.

'Don't talk when you're eating,' she told him. 'Because Lola's mum, Annette, is a production assistant for Sunrise TV, and she's offered to edit these tapes into one half-hour video with proper, professional titles, backing music and everything.' Carefully, Beth deposited the videos into Tom's bag. 'Don't forget to give them to Lola, OK!'

Tom did a runner before she could land any more errands on him.

'By the way,' she called after him. 'Have you thought about buying a birthday present for your dad...?'

Tom was out of there. 'Yeah, birdseed!' he yelled over his shoulder. For Chippie and the rest of Harry's budgies in the shed. The birds deserved a treat.

Chip-chip-chippety-chip! Happy birthday to you!

'Hey, Kyle! Hey, Kalid! Hey, Kingsley!' Tom greeted his mates in the playground. He slung his bag into a corner and joined in the footie match on Jimmy Black's side.

'Here, Tom, pass to me!' Lola called from out on the right wing.

'Whoof!' He booted the ball to Lola, who dribbled past Ryan, then passed to Jimmy. Jimmy's magic left foot beat Kalid in goal.

'One-nil!' Tom's side pranced up and down the playground, hands in the air.

Then the bell went, and the glory faded.

'Hurry, or you'll be late for Registration!' Miss Ambler called, her long skirt blowing in the wind.

As the kids ran to pick up their bags, Tom collided, head-to-head, with Lola.

'Watch it!' she cried.

'Look out!' he yelled back.

'Tom Bean, Lola Kidman, pack it in!' Rambler Ambler shouted from the doorway.

'Whoo-oooh, Tom and Lola!' Danielle trilled as they all charged into school.

'Get lost, Danielle!' they both hissed.

Danielle Hazelwood, Little Miss Stirrer, with her sly, smug grin.

'OK, everyone, sit!' Mr Wright took charge

of the rugby scrum that was meant to be
Registration. 'Kingsley, keep the noise down,
Sasha, come down from the windowsill, and
Kalid, save whatever it is that you're doing
until later!'

Tom slid into his seat and opened up
his bag. Uh-oh, the vids that his mum
had given him were looking a bit bashed.
He decided to offload them onto Lola
before they got any worse. He leaned
across the aisle.

'I've got something for you!' he hissed

at her.

Lola turned. 'Not now, OK? I'm talking to Wayne.'

'Listen, I've gotta give you these!' Tom shoved the three videos across her desk, 'And you've gotta give them to your mum or something.'

'Hey, look at that!' Danielle whispered to Sasha Jones. 'He's lending her his fave vids!'

Tom shot her a dirty look.

'Told you he fancied her!' Danielle giggled. She passed the rumour on from Sasha to Becky Stevens and every other girl in the class.

Whisper-whisper. Tom Bean fancies Lola Kidman!

Blank them, bro,' Kingsley advised, as they escaped from Registration to get changed for their games lesson. 'They'll get over it.'

But Tom felt hot and sticky as he struggled into his football strip. And he blamed his mum for making him pass on those stupid videos, and his dad for having his fiftieth birthday, and the whole world because that's the way it was.

It wasn't until they were out on the pitch, warming up with Leftie Wright, that Tom got back to his normal self.

'OK, teams!' Leftie handed out the coloured bands that divided the class into two. Tom found himself in the red team with Kalid and Lola. 'Today we're turning out for Scotland and Poland in a European Cup semi-final match to be played before a capacity crowd of 90,000! Blues, you're Scotland. Reds, that makes you Poland.'

'And it's captain Kingsley McHarris winning the toss for Scotland!' Kingsley entered into the spirit right away, giving out orders to the Blues, who included Sasha and Danielle. 'C'mon McJones and McHazelwood–get into position!'

'That's the idea!' Leftie grinned. 'And Mot Neabski, you're captain of Poland. Who are you going to put in goal?'

'Alol Namdikski!' Tom decided. 'And Dilak, you play in defence.'

Lola and Kalid trotted to the far end of the pitch.

'Huh? I don't get it,' Ryan complained.

So Tom, his baggy shorts fluttering in the breeze, explained.

'You're Nayr Sdoowski–that's Ryan Woods spelt backwards, with a "ski" on the end!'

'Cool!' Ryan grinned. 'Where d'you want me to play?'

Soon all the Mcs and skis had taken up position and play began.

'And it's Poland's star striker, Neabski, making a run down the centre of the pitch!' Leftie cried. 'But he's stopped by a tackle from McHarris, who makes a long pass ahead to McJones, and now it's Poland's goal mouth under threat...Oh and Polish keeper Namdikski makes a magnificent save off the boot of McHazelwood...!'

The Reds gathered round Lola to

ALOL NAMDIKSI

congratulate her, and Tom patted her on the shoulder.

'Whoo-ooh!' Danielle cooed, before McHarris took the corner kick and threatened the goal mouth once more.

'...And after a tightly fought match, the final score is 2–2!' Leftie announced at the end of the lesson. Player of the Match Award goes to Alol Namdikski, for three breathtaking saves under pressure!'

Lola ran up to receive a Snickers bar.

'Well done, everyone!' the teacher said. 'The replay will take place next week. Same time, same place!'

'This is getting really annoying!' Tom sighed over his apple crumble.

'What is?' Kalid glanced in the direction of Danielle's table, where a bunch of girls were whispering and giggling.

'I don't even LIKE Lola Kidman!'

All morning they'd been going on about it, whoo-oohing and talking behind his back. In Numeracy Hour, Danielle had snuck to the front of the class and chalked 'Tom luvs Lola' on the board. At break, she and Sasha had deliberately shoved Lola against him in the corridor.

'Lola's cool,' Kalid argued. 'She swims, she plays footie, she's a good skateboarding dude. What's not to like?'

'All right, then, I don't FANCY her!' Tom said grudgingly.

'Who don't you fancy, Tom?' It was his mum, who had appeared at his shoulder. She was wheeling a trolley loaded with dirty plates into the kitchen.

'No one!' He frowned and pushed his dish away.

'What's up, love? Are you feeling poorly?'

Beth asked, with a twinkle in her eye.

'No! Why?'

'Well, you haven't eaten all of your pudding, so I thought something must be up.

Tom blushed. It was mega embarrassing having a mum who worked in the school. He knew Danielle's table was overhearing every word.

'It must be lurve, if it's affecting your appetite!' Beth teased.

'Shurrup, Mum!'

'Oh, by the way, did you give Lola those videos?' she asked.

Danielle's table chittered and cheaped like a shed full of budgies. 'Lola...videos... presents...TRUE LURVE!'

Tom groaned. That was it. The final straw. He stood up and raised his voice. 'I don't FANCY anyone, OK!' I never have fancied anyone in this school-not now, not ever!'

There was a mega silence, except for knives and forks clattering in the canteen kitchen.

'Not now, not ever!' Tom's words echoed around the hall. They rose to the ceiling and swooped down through the beams, settling on Danielle's table.

'See!' Danielle hissed loudly. 'What did I tell you. Tom Bean does fancy Lola Kidman–otherwise, why would he bother to deny it?'

Tom wished girls didn't exist. The world should be full of male footballers called Robbie and Jamie, or skateboarding dudes from the US and Oz. You should be able to take exams in grinding, twisting, flicking, flipping, spinning, clunking, whirring, tilting, balancing, flexing...

'Wake up, Tom!' Mr Wright broke into his daydream at the end of the day. 'Are you staying here all night, or going home with the others?'

Tom scrambled for the door.

'Lola said she'd wait for you at the gate,'

Leftie added quietly.

Screech! Tom put on the brakes.
'She never!'

'No, I'm kidding.' Leftie had obviously picked up on the school gossip and was winding Tom up. Don't worry, you're quite safe.'

'Phew!'

Leftie grinned. 'Girls, huh?'

'Yeah.' Tom blushed.

'I hear Robbie Exley's out with a knee injury. That's bad news for the Steelers at this stage in the season.' They talked football as they walked down the corridor, past Bernie King with his fat bulldog, Lennox.

Slop-slop-slop! The caretaker swished water over the floor with a mop.

Slurp slurp slurp! Thirsty Lennox lapped it up.

Yuck! Tom's lip curled in disgust. He and Fat Lennox didn't get on, ever since the dog had tripped him up and sent his skateboard crashing into Bernie King's basement.

'Mind my clean floor!' Bernie growled at Tom.

So Tom took a running jump and cleared the wet patch, while Leftie tiptoed across.

Slop-slop, the caretaker moved on down the corridor.

'Try to stay out of trouble, eh?' the teacher suggested before he and Tom split up. Leftie was heading for his motorbike, crash helmet under his arm.

'Sure!' As if Tom ever caused any problems! 'I've been OK so far this week, haven't I?' No fighting, no being late or making things up...stuff that usually gets up teachers' noses.

'It's only Monday!' Leftie reminded him. 'Let's try and go a whole week without a complaint from Miss Ambler, or any of the other staff, OK?'

Tom nodded. 'Deal!' It'd be tough, but he'd give it his best shot!

Three

'Hi, Annette? It's Beth Bean here.'

Tom could hear his mum whispering down the phone as he set out for the park that evening.

'Listen, I'm having to talk quietly because Harry's out in the garden, and I don't want to risk him overhearing...But the thing is, I've come across another video that we might be able to use on the birthday compilation. D'you mind if I send Tom over to your house with it?'

I'm outta here! Tom lunged for his board and scooted past.

Beth collared him with one hand. 'OK, thanks Annette. I'll send him right now!'

'I can't. I'm meeting Kingsley!'

'Later!' His mum insisted. 'This is important. It's for your dad's big day!'

Tom squeaked and squealed, but it made no difference. Beth popped the video in a bag and ordered him to go straight there and back.

'Whassup, Tom?' Harry emerged from the shed as Tom slunk by.

'Nothin',' Tom said, with a sniff. He felt his mum's eagle eye on him from the kitchen window.

His dad closed the door on his budgies and strolled over for a chat. 'What's that you're carrying? A book?'

'Er...No...a vid.'

'What's the film?'

'Skateboarding!' Tom said, quick as
a flash.

'I might have guessed.' Harry grinned.
'So, how's things?'

'Cool.' Tom itched to get this errand over
with so he could get down to the park. He
reckoned he could skate to the Kidmans'
house and back again in under ten minutes.

But it was a warm, sunny evening for

once, and his dad was in no hurry. 'Played any footie today?' he asked.

'Yeah, we had Games with Mr Wright. I was Mot Neabski and I captained Poland to a 2–2 draw with Scotland.'

'I like that young teacher of yours,' Harry commented. 'Good sense of humour. He sounds like someone I could happily have a beer with.'

Tom saw his mum mouthing things through the window and flapping her hand. 'Go!' she insisted.

'I'm off,' Tom told his dad. 'Mum's hassling me.'

Out of the gate, slamming the board down on the pavement–let's roll!

Tom struck a cool pose down Hammett Street, regularly switching his stance to goofy and back again. He pulled a few fakies and then a perfect ollie.

'Oi! Watch it, you little vandal!' A short man stepped out of his silver Audi TT on to the pavement.

Tom swerved past. There was no law against skateboarding in this area! The dude must be blind not to have seen Tom coming. But giving him verbal would cause an argument and hold Tom up, so he skated on. Past the park, up Margaret Street, along Florence Street to number 44. Tom bailed at the gate and ran up the path to ring the doorbell.

'Hi, Tom!' Lola answered the door dressed in her Nike skateboarding top and trousers. 'Mum, Tom's here with the vid!' she called.

As Annette Kidman made her way down the hall, Tom felt a flush creep up his neck and into his cheeks. He'd hoped that Lola would be out, that he quickly drop the video with her mum and scarper. But no; Lola was grinning at him in a weird way, looking kind of sideways around the edge of the door.

'Tom. Come in!' Annette Kidman ushered him into the hall. She was Lola's double–wild, dark hair, and sporty-looking.

'It's OK, I'm am off to the park...thanks.'
Tom faltered, edging back to the front
doorstep.

'I'll come, too!' Lola said suddenly. She
jammed on her cap and leaped out,
skateboard under her arm.

'Be back in an hour,' Annette told her,
disappearing again inside the house.

Gruesome or what! No way did he want
to turn up at the park with Lola trailing
along behind. 'I'm not goin' straight to the
park,' Tom muttered. 'I have to call in at my
place first.'

'I don't mind,' Lola assured him, smiling.
'I'll come with you.'

What was that weird glint in her eye,
and what did the soppy smile mean? Tom
shuddered and backed away. 'It's OK,' he
mumbled, slamming down his board.

'No, really, I don't mind waiting!' Lola
skated breezily alongside Tom, every now
and then flashing him a sickly grin.

'What's wrong with your face?' Tom

wanted to ask her, but didn't. Instead he
tried every tactic he could think of to out-
skate Lola and leave her behind.

He pulled a crooked grind along the kerb
down Florence Street, and a goofy heelflip
up a car-park ramp into Margaret Street.

Close behind him came the telltale
rumble of Lola's trucks, so Tom gathered
speed. He weaved between bikes and

pushchairs, following a rad line on to Hammett Street.

Lola whirred in hot pursuit. 'Gnarly!' she gasped, as they bailed at Tom's gate.

'Wait here!' Tom ordered, slipping inside the house to check in with his mum, then straight away nipping through the back door to give Lola the slip.

But she must have heard the door slam, because she was round the back to meet him, smiling like a Cheshire cat. 'Boo!' she cried. 'You didn't think you could get rid of me that easily, did you?'

Tom glared back. 'What's the matter with you? Why are you acting weird!?'

'Don't know what you mean,' she simpered.

'Following me, and smiling and stuff!'

'Sorry–don't know what you're on about. I'm only coming skating with you.' Tossing her black mane, Lola stuck her nose in the air.

'Exactly!' Tom saw that he had to spell it

out, word by word. 'With me. That's just it. If you arrive in the park with me, and kids see us, they'll think that stupid Danielle is telling the truth! You and me...together...right!'

Lola fluttered her eyelids like mad. 'So?'

'So, I DON'T fancy you!'

'Very nice, Tom!' Nick rode his bike out of the yard and did a wheelie off the pavement into the road. 'You sure know how to pull the chicks!'

'Get lost!' a furious Tom yelled after him.

'Are you sure you don't fancy me?' Lola batted her lids again, and smiled her sickly smile.

'Double, double, double sure!' Tom insisted. He felt like he was being suffocated by a big, invisible duvet, and he couldn't throw it off to get any fresh air.

'Pity.' Lola sidled closer. 'Cos I've been thinking about what Danielle said earlier today, and I decided I wouldn't mind if you did.'

'Did what?' Tom suddenly felt faint. His eyes were practically bugging out of their sockets.

'Did fancy me,' she giggled.

Tom dropped his board with a crash. 'I DON'T, DO NOT, NEVER DID, NEVER WILL FANCY YOU!'

'Shame,' Lola sighed. She picked up Tom's board and carefully handed it back to him. 'Because, as it happens, Tom Bean, I do fancy you!'

Major earthquake alert! Run for shelter! Lola Kidman fancies me!

Tom was so shocked he abandoned his trip to the park and took refuge in his dad's shed.

'I have to hide and work out what to do,' he confided in Chippie, his budgie friend. 'I mean, this has never happened before.

'Who's a cheeky boy! Where's Thomas? Chip-chip-chippety-chip!' Twenty other budgies fluttered from perch to perch, or clung to the wire-netting partitions, pecking at portions of cuttlefish.

'Help me!' Tom pleaded, as Chippie hopped from his shoulder to the top of his head.

Stay cool, dude, Chippie advised, busily pecking at the peak of Tom's cap. *Who is this chick, anyway?*

'It's Lola Kidman I'm talking about! One of the crew!'

Not some frilly, glittery, girly type, then?

'Right! I thought Lola was cool – swimming and skating and stuff. I never guessed she'd do this to me!'

Gotcha, dude. She crept up on you without warning. It happens. The budgie reappeared on Tom's shoulder and nibbled his earlobe in sympathy.

'Now it's not even safe to go skating in the park, in case Lola shows me up in front of the rest.'

Bummer.

'So how will I get to be a pro, if I

can't practise?'

Tom saw his life's dream fade away. No more massive airs, or defying gravity with speeding wallrides. No more flipping the board in impossible directions in the famous, sun-drenched skate parks of California and Queensland.

Chippie spread his grey-speckled wings and flew to a nearby perch. He fixed Tom with his beady eye. *So you gonna give up ripping and shredding, just like that?*

'What else can I do?' Tom was in despair. 'I have to keep out of Lola's way, in case she grabs me. It means giving up going out. I might even have to change schools!'

You gonna let some girl wreck your whole life?

'Looks like it,' Tom muttered. A fat lot of help Chippie had been! He hunched his shoulders, put on his shades, and walked out of the shed.

Where's Thomas? Who's a cheeky boy! Chippie squawked. *Slam!* went the door.

Tom spent all Tuesday and Wednesday
hiding from Little Miss Superglue.

'Coo-ee, Tom!' she would call from across
the playground, and his heart would sink.
He would pretend to be deaf and walk the
other way. But then she would speed up to
him to show him her latest sticker, or ask

him how come he hadn't shown up in the park the night before.

'Ah, cute!' Danielle and Sasha would sigh. 'Look at Tom and Lola, they're in lurve!'

Or else Lola would collar him after a lesson and bend his ear with how her mum was getting on with the birthday compilation video. 'She's chosen the best extracts and started putting them all on to tape,' she told him. 'You should see the bits of you when you were little, Tom. They're really sweet!'

Yuck! Tom would squirm and scarper. He couldn't bear that sickly voice or those big, fluttery eyes!

'Tough, huh?' Leftie said to him once, when no one else could hear

'Hey, Tom!' Lola would spy him from a mile away-in the park, in the swimming pool, across the soccer pitch. In fact, everywhere he went, Lola would be sure to pop up. 'Tom, I wanna show you something!...Tom, I've learned a gnarly

new trick!...I've bought you a doughnut,
a sticker...Hey, d'you want a piece of gum?'

'Bless!' Sasha and Danielle would coo,
heads together, then bursting into
unstoppable giggles.

Two days of dodging, hopping on buses
and hiding behind walls had worn Tom out.
And still Lola stuck to him.

'Tom, Lola's at the door!' Beth called up
the stairs early on Thursday morning.

Tom was brushing his teeth. In his
surprise, he spat the foam straight at the
mirror–'Puh!'

'Tom!' his mum yelled, louder than
before.

He looked wildly round the bathroom.
No way did he plan to walk into school
with Superglue! Instead, he squeezed
through the tiny window onto the lean-to
roof of the kitchen.

'Tom, where are you?' Beth came up
the stairs.

He slid down the slates to the gutter,

eased himself over the edge and dropped
to the ground. Then he scooted out of the
back gate, cut down the alleyway and
legged it to the bus stop. He was minus his
bag and his tie, but he'd given Lola the slip
for once.

Or so he thought. He was sitting on the
back seat of the bus with Kingsley and
Ryan. They'd pulled up at a traffic light
and were discussing the Steelers' move to
buy Ardilo from Real Madrid for three
million, when suddenly a car horn hooted
beside them.

A quick glance told Tom that it was Lola
Kidman in her mum's yellow Beetle. He
ducked, but Lola pressed the horn again.

'It's no good, she's seen you,' Ryan
told him.

So Tom peered out. Lola grinned and
waved his red-and-white tie at him. 'You
forgot this!' she mouthed, before the lights
turned green and the traffic eased forward.

And she was there at the school gate

before him, holding out the tie and his bag. 'Waymann would have killed you if she'd seen you without this,' she told him. 'Good job your mum noticed it and gave it to me when I called for you.'

Miss Ambler, who was nearby, noticed Lola's kindly action. 'Say thank you to Lola,' she reminded Tom, sharply.

He grabbed the tie, wishing he could throttle Lola with it. 'Thanks,' he muttered. *Thanks for nothing. Thanks for being the worst thing that ever happened to me, full stop!*

Four

'It's no good, you know.' Lola had chosen
Tom's walk home from school on Thursday
teatime to corner him yet again. She'd
waited until Tom had split off from Kalid
at the corner of Hammett Street, then
pounced.

'Erck!' Tom's shattered nerves made him
jump a mile. 'What's no good?' he gasped,
backed up against a tall brick wall.

'There's no point in you running away and hiding.' Lola faced him.

'Get lost, Lola!' he told her straight. 'For the last time, I don't fancy you, OK!'

Lola boxed him tighter into a corner. There was a giant poster advertising a BMW Z3 behind him, and a newsagent's to one side. 'That's not the point,' she explained. 'I want you to be my boyfriend anyway.'

'You can't force me!' he squeaked. Major panic. There was a new, harsh glint in Lola's eye that he didn't like.

'Listen,' she said. I'm fed up of following you everywhere, being nice to you...'

'Good!' he cried. At last there was a flicker of hope.

'So I've no choice but to resort to drastic action.'

Puff! The flame went out. Tom was left in the dark. 'Get lost!' he told her again, ducking and escaping from the corner. He was ten metres down the street before she

called him back. 'I know something about you!' she said in a sing-song voice. 'Something that you wouldn't want anyone else to know about!'

Tom braked and turned. 'What?' he shot back.

Lola sauntered towards him, hands on hips. 'Something secret!'

Tom's life flashed before him. What

secret? Was it the time he'd broken the corner on a coffee table and glued it back together without his mum or dad noticing? Or the time a week earlier, when he'd played a trick on Leftie by sticking gum to the seat of his chair? No one had any proof that it was him, Tom Bean, who'd done it. Except, maybe, Lola-if she'd been secretly spying on him. 'What secret?' he demanded.

Lola came up close. 'Oh, just something I saw on your mum's video,' she whispered.

Tom frowned. So it was a family secret. Lola had obviously been watching all the tapes as her mum edited them. She must have picked up some embarrassing detail to bribe him with. But what could be that embarrassing?

'Yeah, well, tough!' he retorted. 'Go ahead and tell people. I don't care!'

He was two strides away, toughing it out, when Lola spoke again. 'You will care, Tom Bean!' she warned. 'When you find out what it is.'

His stride faltered. What if it was something mega? Something he'd forgotten about that could destroy his gnarly reputation? Could he risk it?

'Don't you wanna know?' she teased.

'Yeah. Spit it out, why don't you?'

But after three days of being snubbed. Lola was going to make Tom sweat. 'Come to my house at six o'clock tonight,' she told him, her eyes narrowing and her voice hardening. 'Then you can see for yourself...'

Dude, you're between a rock and a hard place! Chippie saw Tom's problem straight away. *If you go to the chick's pad, it looks like you're an item. If you stay away, she spills the beans.*

Tom nodded. 'It's blackmail. That's what it is!'

The way I see it, you gotta go. The bird gave it to Tom straight. *Find out what the secret is. Play her along, then dump her!*

At least it was a plan.

'Tom, what's the matter with you? Have you got ants in your pants?' Harry Bean asked at tea. He'd noticed his youngest son pushing his food around his plate and fidgeting on his chair.

'Can I go to the park, now, please?' Tom begged.

'Not until you've eaten your fish pie,' Beth insisted. 'You're skinny enough already, without missing meals.'

'I'll have his!' Nick offered, scooping a spoonful from Tom's plate.

'Nick!' Harry warned.

Meanwhile, Tom shovelled down the last of his potato and cod mush. 'Finished! Can I go now?'

'Yes–go before you wear out the floor

with your chair legs!' Beth sighed. 'And, thank you, Mum, for another wonderful meal!'

Tom grunted his thanks and raced out. He didn't even stop to grab his board, but instead sprinted to Florence Street on foot. He arrived at Lola's house, out of breath and full of churned up fish pie, and spotted her at an upstairs window. Before he could get his breath back, she was opening the door and letting him in.

'I knew you'd come,' she crowed. 'Couldn't resist me, huh?'

'Cut it out,' he muttered. 'Just show me the vid.'

'Wait here. I'll have to ask Mum.' Quickly Lola disappeared, leaving Tom in the hall. She came back with Annette in tow.

'Hi, Tom! Nice to see you.' Annette's welcome was warm and genuine. 'Lola tells me you want a sneak preview of Saturday's tape?'

He nodded, not trusting himself to speak.

The churning in his stomach was getting worse, probably due to nerves and him running all the way here.

'Well, it's not quite finished yet. I still have to add titles and some soundtrack, but you can look at it if you like. It's ready and waiting in the machine. Just press Start.'

Stumbling behind Lola into the Kidmans' living room, Tom stood awkwardly by the door.

'Sit down, I won't bite,' Lola promised, settling down on the big sofa with the remote control.

Tom wafted his hot face. His stomach churned like a washing machine, then a big bubble of air escaped and made its way up to his gullet. 'Barp!'

Lola wrinked her nose. 'Ergh! Tom! Gross!'

Tom saw his chance. 'Yeah, gross. Have you gone off me?' He was halfway through the door before she called him back.

'Hold it!' Lola ordered. 'You don't get out

of it that easy!' She pressed Play and made him watch.

There was all the usual family stuff, beginning with black and white photographs of Beth and Harry's wedding.

'Guess they didn't have videos back in the old days,' Lola commented.

There was nothing so far that looked too worrying to Tom. Just baby pics of Mike and Robert, early 35millimetre film of a holiday in Corfu, a section on Nick's christening, then a family Christmas before Tom was born.

Boring! Tom yawned and looked at his watch.

'You may be yawning now.' Lola smirked. 'But wait till you see what's coming next!'

'Summer 1999!' Harry Bean's voice announced. 'The Beans have moved bang up to date with a new camcorder for their trip to Florida. Here's us getting off the plane at Orlando Airport. This is our hotel, just outside Disneyland. And this is Beth,

Tom and Nick meeting Mickey Mouse!'

Tom stared at his younger self. He had a bad haircut and sticky-out ears, and orange trainers with soles that flashed. But still, nothing that would give Lola a definite hold over him.

'And here's our Tom dressed up as a dwarf!' Harry announced.

Tom's jaw dropped. How could he have forgotten dressing up as Dopey for *Snow White and the Seven Dwarves*? He must have blanked it out, made himself forget the whole humiliating episode.

'I'll just rewind and play that bit again,' Lola said sweetly.

'...And here's our Tom dressed up as a dwarf!' Harry's voice repeated.

Pause.

Tom was fixed in the

frame, wearing a long, yellow nightie thing, with red pointy shoes. On his head was a floppy knitted cap, which forced his ears to curve forwards. And he stood in line with six other dwarves, carrying shovels and singing, *'Heigh-ho! Heigh-ho! It's off to work we go!'* Tom was a Disney dwarf called Dopey, and living up to his name!

Lola pressed Play again.

'Heigh-ho! Heigh-ho!
It's off to work we go!
With a rom-pom-pom
And a rom-pom-pom
Heigh-ho! Heigh-ho! Heigh-ho! Heigh-ho!'

'OK, OK.' Tom gave in. He couldn't watch any more. Not the bit where he came up, stood on tiptoe, and kissed Snow White on the cheek. Nor the part where he grinned his goofy, toothless grin at the camera. Being Dopey was something he had never admitted to anyone. His mum had forced him into it, and now it had come back to haunt him.

Lola pressed Stop. 'Now will you be my boyfriend?' she demanded.

'Yes!' he agreed. 'Anything! As long as you promise not to tell a single living soul!'

'Sit next to me, Tom!' Lola invited at the start of the art lesson. She patted the empty chair, then made space on the table.

Tom screwed up his face and sat.

'Tom 4 Lola!' Danielle scribbled on his paper before he began to paint...

'Be my partner, Tom!' Lola cried during Drama.

They had to make up a dance, pretending to be waves crashing on to the shore.

'Whose stupid idea was this?' Tom muttered, as Miss Ambler clashed a cymbal and they threw themselves to the floor.

Lola rolled alongside and giggled. 'Yeah, naff idea!' she agreed.

'Lola + Tom = Luv!' Sasha traced the words with her finger on the steamed up changing-room window...

'You coming to play footie after dinner?' Ryan asked Tom as they queued in the school cafeteria.

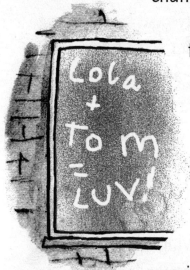

Tom had to check with Lola. 'Are we?'

'You bet!' she grinned, as if to say that being in love didn't stop people playing footie.

But she had to be on Tom's side, and hug him when he scored.

'Tom for Lola, Lola for Tom, ra-ra-ra!' Danielle and Sasha chanted, cheer-leading style. They marched up and down the touchline, shouting at the tops of their voices...

'Are you OK, Tom?' Leftie asked him during private reading–when Lola had insisted on sharing Tom's book.

'Yep,' he said, miserably, meaning, *No! Help! I can't stand it!*

'Next time, remember to bring your own book, Lola,' Leftie remarked before he walked on...

'See you tonight, then,' Lola told Tom. She walked Tom home and stopped at his garden gate.

'What time?' he said wearily. All day Kingsley had been giving him funny looks, as if to say, 'How come you're cosying up with Lola instead of sticking with the crew?'

'Half-six, down in the park,' she replied, swinging her bag and singing as she skipped off along the street.

'This is Lidar, my magic laser sword!' Tom held up his dad's golf club in front of his bedroom mirror. 'With this ray I can exterminate my enemies. Its deadly light cuts through walls of rock and turns the sea to ice. It can transport me into the future and blast me back into the past.

With this sword, I am all-powerful!'

He stood boldly, feet apart, the sword raised above his head. With Lidar, he could surround Lola with rays that turned her into a statue and sent her hurtling into outer space. Yeah, if only...

OK, if magic was out of the question, there must be other ways. Maybe in real life he could fix up an accident–not a bad one, just enough to put Lola out of action for a week or two. He could trip her up with his foot and she could sprain her ankle. He could give her ice cream that was past its sell-by date and give her a stomach ache, and her mum would have to call the doctor.

Then again, perhaps he could persuade Kalid to fancy Lola instead. Yeah, Kalid was the type girls liked–dead smiley, with loads of funny jokes. If Kalid took on the job of being Lola's boyfriend, then Tom would be free...

'Tom, Lola's here!' Harry called from downstairs.

Tom looked at his watch and groaned. Thirty-three minutes past six.

'You're late!' Lola yelled.

'Yeah, coming!' he yelled back.

He ran down in his shades and picked up his board.

'Happy birthday for tomorrow, Mr Bean!' Lola told a bemused Harry. 'Are you doing anything spesh?' she added, innocently.

'No, I don't think so,' Harry replied. 'Just a quiet day at home, watching Sky Sport.'

'Well, have a really cool day!' she said, grabbing Tom by the arm and dashing off.

'You'd better not say anything to Dad,' Tom warned. All week his mum had worked at keeping the birthday extravaganza a surprise.

'Don't worry, I won't,' Lola promised. 'I want to see the look on his face when he realises what's happening!'

Tom stopped and stared. 'You mean, you'll be at the party?' he wailed.

Lola laughed at his panic-stricken face. 'Yeah, Mum and me have been invited, too. I wouldn't miss your dad's surprise party for anything!'

Five

'Cake, candles, sandwiches, nibbles...' Beth ticked off items from her list. 'Nick, I want you out of that bathroom so that I can give it a good clean. Tom, your skateboard's lethal in the hallway, so move it where people can't trip over it!'

Tom was deep into a Misled Youth video of two black kids called Chad and Aaron skating a bump-to-shopping-trolley-rack.

Chad ollied it, while Aaron threw a rad backside flip over it. 'Insane!' Tom murmured.

'Tom! Move your board and clear up your room!' Beth insisted. 'We have to be ready for this party by two o'clock, when your dad comes home from work.' She swept into the living-room and turfed Tom off the sofa. 'What are all those pebbles doing at the top of the stairs?'

'They're fossils, 'Tom grunted. He'd collected them yonks ago, on a day trip to the seaside. All he needed was a hammer to bash them apart and discover the prehistoric thingummies inside.

'Throw them out!' Beth handed him an empty bin bag. 'And tidy your room!'

Tom stomped upstairs. From the kitchen came the smell of grilled sausages and stuff in the oven. In the bathroom, Nick and the shower were still in full flow.

'Aren't you clean enough for Zoe yet?' Tom scoffed through the door. 'Don't forget your whiffy armpits!'

Nick ignored him, so Tom stooped to collect the pebbles and chuck them in the bin bag–clunk-clunk. But as soon as he picked the bag up, the pebbles dropped straight through the bottom.

'Chocolate biscuits, crisps, cheese straws, peanuts...' Beth ran from room to room, carrying dishes of nibbles. 'Someone, please blow up those balloons!' she pleaded.

Tom ditched the clearing up and jumped the flight of stairs in one go. 'Supermaa-an! How many?'

'As many as you can manage. Let's aim for fifty.'

Tom started blowing, waiting for that moment when the tiny round sack suddenly expanded, and the air from his lungs pumped it up to its full, see-through size. One-two-three-four-five...Phew, his cheeks were aching and the insides of his mouth were tingling...Six-seven-eight-nine...and he ran out of puff.

'Why can't we have helium ones?' he asked.

'Because!' his mum answered. mid-Hoover.

Vroooom, the cleaner droned over the carpets, sucking up crumbs, paperclips, fluff and shoelaces.

By one o'clock the house was tidy and the party food was set out on plates in the kitchen and living-room. Nick was busy with aftershave and hair gel, and while Beth was getting changed out of her jeans into a posh frock, Tom wolfed down two sausages and a chocolate finger.

At one-thirty, guests began to arrive. First was Tom's oldest brother, Robert, with his wife, Sal. Rob looked cool in a new hoodie, shaved head and a stud earring. Sal wore a skirt that showed most of her legs. 'We brought some CDs, where's the player?' Sal asked.

Then Mike, Tom's other brother, showed up with two of his mates from college.

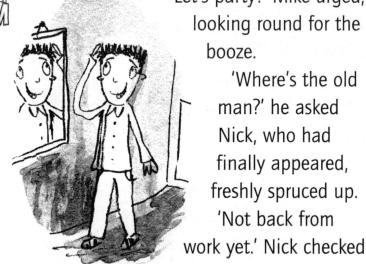

'Let's party!' Mike urged, looking round for the booze.

'Where's the old man?' he asked Nick, who had finally appeared, freshly spruced up.

'Not back from work yet.' Nick checked his hair spikes in the hall mirror, then went to meet Zoe.

Meanwhile, Beth appeared in her red party dress and high heels, wearing make-up and a gold necklace.

Rob and Mike overdid the wolf-whistles as she came downstairs.

'Yeah, whatever!' she said with a pleased blush.

The Beans' house started filling up with people. Kingsley arrived with his dad, Wesley, and his mum, Victoria. The Hills from next door called by with a present, then stayed for drinks. Dave and Alice Hazelwood brought Danielle, dressed in a silver top and a denim skirt. Wayne Penny showed up with his mum, Jo. Plus there were loads of grown-ups who Tom didn't know.

All he knew was, the crisps were disappearing fast and he needed some air. So he, Kingsley and Wayne grabbed a handful of nibbles each, and shuffled towards the back door.

'Not so fast!' Beth stopped them in their tracks. 'You'll give the game away when your dad arrives,' she told Tom. 'We have to stay inside and wait.'

It was nearly two o'clock and thirty people were crammed into the Beans' house. Annette and Lola made it just in time.

'Sorry we're late!' Annette cried. 'I was putting the final touches to the video.'

The video! Tom's heart lurched. The trip to Disneyland and Tom's starring role!

How thick could he be? Tom closed his eyes and felt his head spin. He'd done the deal with Lola and completely forgotten that the evidence still existed. Everyone would know now, anyway! Him as Dopey, with his gap-toothed grin and sticky-out ears. In fact, it was here now, being handed to Beth by Annette, with Lola standing there, the picture of innocence. Ergh!

'What's up, Heinz?' Kingsley asked. 'You look weird.'

'I'm fine!' Tom tried to act normal. Meanwhile he felt his heart speed up and sweat beads form on his top lip. 'I'll take the video!' he offered, almost tripping in his rush to get at it.

'Oh no you won't,' Beth countered. 'This is precious, I'll hang on to it myself, thanks very much!'

Lola was smiling sweetly. 'Hey, Tom. D'you like my silver scrunchie?' She turned the back of her head to him so that he could judge the full effect.

Before he had time to answer there was a cry from Sal at the window. 'Harry's here!' And everyone fell silent.

Tom's dad parked his car at the front of the house. He paused a moment to glance down the street and wave at someone in the distance. Then he took off his work jacket and sauntered up the path.

'Ssshhh!' Beth warned.

Thirty squashed guests held their breath.

Harry's key turned in the lock and he stepped inside.

'Surprise!' everyone cried. Mike and Rob released a shower of balloons from the top landing. 'Happy birthday, Harry!'

Tom watched his dad's face. It went from normal, to shock, to laughing, in a nano second. Then Harry saw Beth, grabbed her, and gave her a big hug.

'Happy birthday to you!' everyone sang, crowding round and cheering.

'You don't look a day over seventy!'

'Fifty years young!'

'Half a century!'

'Come and rest your legs, you poor old geezer!'

Then it was party time proper, with corks popping, people cheering, music blasting, and present-opening. There was wrapping paper everywhere, lots of smiles, and a few tears from Beth.

'Why is your mum crying?' Kingsley asked.

'Because she's happy, dummy!' Danielle told him,

'Then why isn't Harry crying?' Kingsley persisted.

Danielle raised her eyes at Lola and tutted. *Boys!*

'More music!' Sal cried, changing the CD. 'Everybody boogie!'

'Dance with me, Tom!' Lola seized his hand and led Tom, cringing, into the living-room. 'Like this...,' She demonstrated, hand on waist, one finger in the air.' Wiggle your hips!'

No way! Tom did a runner between Zoe and Nick, over the back of the sofa and through the door.

A stranded Lola frowned, then followed him into the kitchen. 'If you don't dance with me I'll tell everyone your secret!'

'Go ahead!' Tom was past caring. It would only be a matter of minutes before they played the lousy video and the whole thing would be out in the open. Kingsley would know. Wayne would know. And Dobber Danielle. It had all been for nothing. 'I wish I'd never agreed to be your boyfriend!' he yelled at Lola. 'It was a stupid idea in the first place!'

'Uh-oh–lover's tiff?' Danielle poked her head round the door. 'Is there anything I can do?'

'Yes, get lost!' Tom and Lola screeched together.

And Danielle disappeared with a giggle.

'To-om,' Lola began, looking at him from under her long, dark lashes. 'I know you don't really mean this...'

'Yeah, I do!' Suddenly Tom saw a way out of the whole mess. It was dead simple, staring him in the face all along. He hadn't been thinking straight.

'But I thought we were getting on fine.' Lola's frown deepened. 'We both like footie and skateboarding, don't we?'

'Yeah, but I hate dancing,' Tom pointed out. 'And I don't want a girlfriend, full stop, with knobs on!'

'Oh.'

For a second, Tom thought it was Lola's turn to blub. 'You shouldn't have blackmailed me,' he muttered.

'Are you dumping me?' Lola challenged him, drying her eyes and facing him full-on.

Tom nodded. He didn't have time for

long explanations, he had something to do, and fast.

'Then I'll tell everyone. Dopey-Dopey-Dopey!' Lola's taunts rose above the music playing in the next room.

'Go ahead. I'll just deny it. They won't believe you, they'll think you're only saying it because I dumped you!'

'What about the video? Kingsley, Wayne and Danielle are all going to see it. It'll be all round school by Monday!'

Tom held a trump card up his sleeve, which he wasn't about to share with Superglue. He squared his shoulders, ready for action. 'So, it doesn't make any difference then, does it?' He shrugged. 'If they're going to find out anyway?' But secretly, Tom had no intention of letting anyone see him as a dwarf...And he had a cunning plan...

'Easy-peasy!' Tom held up the video to show Kingsley and Wayne.

'Did you nick it?' Wayne whispered from the safety of the shed, where the three boys were hiding out.

Tom nodded. 'Mum had put it down on top of the telly while she lit the candles on Dad's cake. I just snuck in and took it.'

He made it sound simple, but his heart had been banging against his ribs as he'd sidled out of the living-room while everyone watched Harry blow out his fifty candles. No one had noticed him, except for Kingsley and Wayne. They'd followed him out to the garden and demanded to know what was going on. And he had a story all lined up for them...

'It's got stuff on it that I don't want people to see,' he said vaguely.

Wayne ducked as Chippie flew by. 'Where's Thomas?' the bird croaked.

'Such as?' Kingsley asked.

'Y'know, baby pictures, soppy stuff like that.'

'Yeah, gotcha.' Kingsley could easily see

Tom's point. 'The wrinklies are always doing that–showing pics that totally show you up.'

'Who's a cheeky boy? Chip-chippety-chip!'

'Wow, cool!' Wayne gasped at the talking budgie.

'So you won't tell Mum?' Tom checked with Kingsley as he hid the stolen tape under the boxes of bird food at the back of the shed.

'Bro, my lips are totally sealed!' Kingsley promised solemnly. 'That's what mates are for, right?'

Wicked! Chippie agreed. *Yo, dude!*

Six

'Man, I'm stoked!' Kingsley was back inside
the house and enjoying the party. He'd
kicked balloons, trampolined on the sofa,
and won a three-way crisp-eating contest.

'Me, too!' Now that the video nightmare
was solved, Tom didn't have a care in the
world. He raced around with a box of party
poppers, freaking everyone out with the
bangs and cascades of coloured paper.

'Calm down,' Beth warned. 'If you boys wreck the place, I'll make you clean it up afterwards.'

But Tom could see his mum was having too good a time herself to really mean it. The Big Surprise had worked. Now she could enjoy the fun.

'Can we play musical statues?' Tom begged over the sound of loud guitars.

'Not with this head-banging stuff blasting us out of the room!' His mum grinned. 'Come and have another piece of cake before it all gets eaten.'

In the kitchen Tom found his dad happily drinking and chatting with Mike. At six foot three and two, they towered over the other guests, and they had the same laid-back way of joking and kidding along.

'Tom, what's round and yellow with four grey circles?' Rob came up from behind and asked.

'An elephant lying upside down in a bowl of custard,' Tom sighed. *Like everyone knows that stoopid joke!*

'What's black and white, and red all over?' Harry tried to catch Tom out.

'Dunno.'

'A newspaper,' his dad grinned. 'Y'know, "read" all over. Red–read–R-E-A-D!'

Tom curled his lip. 'OK, then. Why did the turkey cross the road?'

Harry, Rob and Mike thought hard.

'Because it was the chicken's day off!' Wayne told them.

Tom belted him over the head with a balloon for stealing his punchline.

'Right. Time for the birthday video!' Beth announced to everyone in the house. 'Make your way into the front room. The show will begin in five minutes.'

Whoops! Tom tried to fade into the background. He wasn't looking forward to the moment when his mum realised that the vid had mysteriously gone missing. Still, if it saved his street cred it was worth it.

'Oh no you don't!' Beth collared him and

dragged him to the living-room with Rob, Mike, Nick and their dad. 'This is a family show! You five are the stars!'

'PG only!' Wesley Harris joked. 'Is it suitable for the under-eights?' There was a buzz of expectation as the guests squeezed into the Bean's living-room.

'Now. Where is that tape?' Beth muttered to herself. 'I'm sure I left it here, on top of the TV...'

Tom snuck a look at Wayne, who was bright red, and at Kingsley, who was whistling quietly and staring at the ceiling.

Tom's mum pressed Eject to check that the tape wasn't already in the machine. Then she fumbled underneath in case it had fallen behind the video recorder. 'That's funny...' she murmured.

Tom's pangs of guilt were getting stronger. His poor mum was panicking now, and it was all down to him. Somehow he felt that accusing eyes were boring into him. Yet how could that be...? Unless

Wayne had snitched! Tom shot another suspicious glance at timid Wayne. Had he dobbed Tom in?

Wayne shook his head. Not guilty!

'Trust me to lose the tape!' Beth started to apologise in an upset voice. She'd been down on her hands and knees, looking under chairs, pushing stray balloons to one side in a vain effort to find the missing vid. 'It was going to be a Complete History of the Bean Family–warts and all!'

'Well, thank heavens you lost it, then!' Harry joked.

'No, it was good. Annette did it for us. It had a proper commentary, titles and everything!' Beth looked as though the whole special day had fallen apart...

...Until Annette Kidman sprang forward. 'Don't panic!' she told everyone, dipping a hand deep into her leather bag. 'Da-dah! A professional TV production assistant always carries a spare–just in case!'

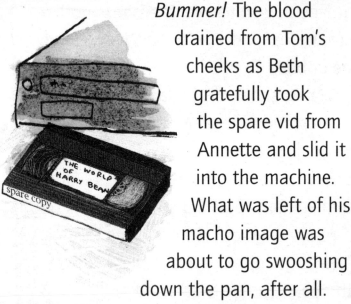

Bummer! The blood drained from Tom's cheeks as Beth gratefully took the spare vid from Annette and slid it into the machine. What was left of his macho image was about to go swooshing down the pan, after all.

'Hang on a sec-time to refill people's glasses before we settle down?' Harry suggested.

Tom felt like a prisoner on Death Row-who had got a last-minute stay of execution. He breathed again.

Then Lola pushed her way to the front and hassled him. 'I expect you thought you'd got away with it, didn't you?' she whispered, dragging Tom into a corner.

'Dunno what you mean,' he sulked.

'Yeah you do. You nicked the first video

so that no one would see you dressed up
as Dopey the Dwarf!'

'D'you blame me?' Tom didn't see any
point in denying it now. He could hear the
loud swishing of water down a toilet bowl,
as his whole life vanished down the drain.

'I could still save you,' Lola hissed into
his ear.

'How?'

Tom's dad and Rob were pouring more drinks. His mum was hovering by the TV.

'Trust me!' Lola eyeballed him. 'But I'll only save you on one condition.'

'Which is?'

'That you promise to keep on being my boyfriend!'

'For how long?' Tom whimpered.

'For ever!' she insisted. 'Otherwise, no deal!'

Tom groaned and shook his head. A lifetime of Miss Superglue. No, no, this was too much!

'Dopey!' Lola reminded him, with that steely glint.

Tom crumpled. 'OK, OK!'

'Cool. This is what we have to do...'

'Ladies and gentlemen!' Wesley Harris had stood up and cleared his throat to make a speech. 'Before we watch the video, I'd like to congratulate Harry on reaching his half-century, not out. I've known Harry for half that time, since we played football together for Woodbridge Town. Harry was a wicked goalkeeper, who could've turned pro if he'd wanted, but that wasn't Harry's style...'

'Got it?' Lola whispered.

Tom nodded. 'This had better work!' he muttered.

'It will, if you do your bit right,' she promised.

'...So, we're all here to say Happy Birthday to Harry, our good mate,' Wesley concluded. 'Cheers, Harry, and many happy returns!'

'Cheers... Happy Birthday, and lots more of 'em!' The shout went up, while Harry Bean stood and raised his pint.

'Mrs Bean, I'll work the remote for you!' Lola volunteered. 'You sit down next to Mr Bean and enjoy the show!'

'Are you sure?' Beth hesitated.

'Yeah, I do it for Mum when she's editing in the studio. No problem!'

So Tom's mum handed over the remote control and joined their guests.

'Action!' Wesley called. 'Let's roll with the Bean Family History–Director's Cut!'

Lola pressed Play and the title appeared. *The World of Harry Bean!* In the background a smoochy voice sang 'I Did It My Way'.

'God, is that you, Harry?' Jo Penny called, when the snapshots of Harry and Beth's wedding appeared onscreen. The tall groom wore a droopy moustache and a wide pink tie.

'If he's marrying my wife, I guess he must be,' Harry kidded.

'You look so different!' Jo gasped.

'Harry's a happy hippy!'

'Love and peace, man!'

Tom hardly heard the rude comments from the audience. Instead he made his way to the window and perched on the sill, his nerves strung out like guitar strings. Now the vid was showing the baby pics of his two older brothers, and people were cooing over them. Next it would be the

holiday in Corfu, then Nick's christening.
Tom took a quick look out of the window
and prayed.

Greek music played over scenes of golden
beaches and blue seas. There was Harry,
being buried up to the neck in sand by Rob
and Mike. Beth was lounging on the beach
in her bikini.

'Then came Nick,' the commentary
announced. And there was a squidgy,
gurgly baby goo-gooing on a mat, then
being dunked in a bath.

Zoe shrieked and hid her face in her
hands.

'After Nick, Harry and Beth took a bit of
a break on the baby front,' Annette's voice
continued. 'And it seems their trusty old
video camera broke down, because the next
we see of the Bean clan is when Tom was
six years old, and the family went Stateside,
to visit Disneyland.

Tom took a deep breath. There was the
whole gang shaking hands with Mickey,

then a parade down a broad street, with
Snow White's castle in the background...

'Dad!' Tom screeched at the top of his
voice. 'Chippie's escaped!' He jumped up in
a panic and pointed wildly through the
window. 'He's got out of the shed, and

now he's flying away!' ('Come up with something that'll distract 'em!' Lola had instructed. 'And make it good!')

The whole room buzzed.

'Oh no, poor Chippie!'

'How did he get out?'

'It's Harry's favourite budgie!'

'Where?' Harry pushed his way to the window to join Tom. Lola fast-forwarded the tape in a blur.

'Oh, no, it's OK!' Tom reported. He sat down as suddenly as he'd sprung up. 'It was just a crisp packet blowing in the wind. I made a mistake. Sorry everyone!'

Giving him a gentle, pretend cuff around the ear, Harry relaxed. 'You had me going there for a moment!'

'Sorry, Dad!' Tom grinned sheepishly. Wow, was he a great actor, or what! Watch out Brad Pitt!

'Heigh-ho! Heigh-ho! Heigh-ho!' Lola re-pressed Play with the strains of Snow White's seven dwarves fading from the soundtrack. The video had moved on to the bit where Harry and Nick stepped off a white-knuckle ride minus their baseball caps and the contents of their popcorn buckets.

'Cor, you look as sick as a parrot, Harry!' Wesley called out. And the audience settled down happily to enjoy the rest of the show.

Seven

'Phew!' After everyone had gone home from the party, Tom gave Chippie the full story. 'It was close, but the plan worked. No one saw the dwarf!'

Cool. The budgie pecked happily at his birdseed. *Glad I could help, dude.*

'I had to think of a mega shock,' Tom explained. 'Maybe me havin' a heart attack or chokin' on a sausage roll. But no, that wouldn't have done it. Not like saying you'd flown the coop!'

Yeah. Me and Harry go back a long way, Chippie agreed.

'Lola only needed about ten seconds to fast forward over Dopey.'

Oh yeah, the chick. What is it with you and her?

'Nothing! Listen, I haven't finished yet. No one noticed Lola press the button except for Annette Kidman. She gave me one of those looks, like, "I know what you're up to, but I won't let on!" '

What about the chick? Chippie insisted. He looked up from his food into a little round mirror dangling from a higher perch. 'Who's a cheeky boy? Chip-chip-chippety-chip!'

The chick. Lola. Tom thought of a new joke. Why did the boy cross the road? To get away from the Superglue Chick!

He shrugged, turned off the light and walked out of the shed. *I'm stuck with her,* he thought, miserably. He should have told the budgie, but he couldn't bear to talk about it. *She knows my guilty secret. Now I have to go out with her for ever and ever!*

'Ooh! My head hurts!' Harry groaned on Sunday morning.

'Don't open the curtains. Leave me alone!' Beth moaned.

Tom left them to it and took his board down the park. He practised some street tricks in blissful peace, until Danielle Hazelwood came past with her Jack Russell terrier.

Yip-yap-yap! The dog attacked Tom's deck.

Tom bailed and rolled in the grass. The dog pounced on him and licked his face.

'Ergh! Yuck! Get 'im off me!' he yelled.

'Here, Toby!' Danielle chirruped.

Lick-lick-more-lick!

'Get 'im off!'

'He's only kissing you!' Danielle

explained. 'I thought you'd be used to that these days!'

'His breath stinks!' Tom bellowed, wrestling the dog and throwing it off.

'Mwah-mwah, kissy-kiss!' Danielle taunted. 'Tom loves Lola, mwah!'

'Get lost!' Tom grabbed his board and ran.

'Whassup?' Kingsley greeted him at the

park gate. He was duded up in shades, a cap and a wicked new pair of Emerica Signature shoes. 'Where are you going?'

'Home!' Tom gasped, pointing back at Danielle and Toby.

'Girl trouble, huh?' Kingsley sympathised. 'You've got your hands full, Tom Bean. I just saw your other girlfriend outside your house. She probably wants to skate with you!'

The news sent Tom into a fresh panic. 'Help!' he cried. 'What am I gonna do?'

'What's the problem? You're one hot dude!' A grin spread over Kingsley's face. 'The girls are freaking out over you, don't ask me why!'

'Well, I'm not freaking out over them!' Tom retorted. He'd reached the limit—the end of his tether. 'I'd rather be Dopey!' he yelled. 'I'm Tom Bean! I'm a dwarf in a yellow nightie and sticky-out ears! I admit it—end of story!' There, he'd done it. The secret was out.

'Dunno what you're talking about, dude.'
Kingsley shrugged. 'All I know is, it's Sunday
and I'm gonna pull some gnarly tricks. See
ya, bye!'

'I feel sick!' Tom clutched his stomach
and bent double over the breakfast table.
'I can't go to school today!'

His mum felt his head and told him he
didn't have a temperature.

So Tom went upstairs, pressed his
forehead against the radiator, and ran
back down. 'Mum, I'm
burning up! I've got
a fever!'

'What are those
red stripes on your
forehead?' Beth
asked with a frown.
'They look
suspiciously like
radiator marks to me.
Only surely not even you,

Tom Bean, would pull a stupid trick like that?'

'Do I have to go to school?' Tom moaned. He'd spent the whole day yesterday hiding from Lola, and last night he'd had nightmares about being kissed by a dog that suddenly turned into a girl.

'Get out of your pyjamas and into your clean uniform,' Beth ordered. 'No messing!'

OK, then, if he was forced to meet Lola face-to-face, he would set about putting her off him. Maybe by being as smelly and grungy as possible?

No washing for a start.

'Go and have a wash!' Beth ordered. 'Use soap and warm water—and don't forget to do behind your ears!'

Tom splished and splashed without touching his face. Then he dived into the linen basket and dragged out last week's uniform. Crumpled shirt and trousers, stained sweater, smelly socks.

Would that be enough? No, he'd better

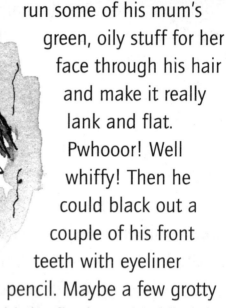

run some of his mum's green, oily stuff for her face through his hair and make it really lank and flat. Pwhooor! Well whiffy! Then he could black out a couple of his front teeth with eyeliner pencil. Maybe a few grotty blackheads to add the final touch-dab-dab-dab with a pencil. Perfect!

'Tom-you're going to be late!' Beth warned.

Tom waited at the top of the stairs until she was out of the way, then he snuck down. 'Bye Mum!' he yelled, as he slammed the front door. Wicked! As he ran for the bus, he felt triple sure that not even Lola Kidman could fancy him looking and smelling like this!

Only one problem-Lola wasn't at school.

'Sasha Jones.' Mr Wright raced through the register.

'Here, sir.'

'Lola Kidman...Lola Kidman?'

Silence.

'Does anyone know where Lola is this morning?'

'Yeah. Tom Bean scared her away!' Ryan Woods sniggered.

Tom glowered from the back row. The green oil in his hair stank, and it was trickling down his forehead. His crumpled clothes gave off a nasty odour, and the fake blackheads had smudged into grubby streaks.

Leftie looked straight at Tom for the first time since he'd entered the classroom. 'Whoah! You're looking a bit rough there, lad!'

Tom's face went redder, and hotter.

'Is that a five o'clock shadow I see on your chin?' Leftie wouldn't let Tom off the hook. He left his desk and strolled down the aisle towards him.

'Lord love us!' The teacher's nostrils quivered as he smelt Tom. 'Have you been rolling in something you shouldn't?'

By this time Ryan, Kalid and Kingsley were cawing with laughter. Danielle, Sasha and the other girls were tittering and whispering.

'No, sir!'

'Then what?' The corners of Leftie's mouth twitched.

'Yeah! Come clean, Tom Bean!' Kalid called out. 'Come clean-geddit!'

Leftie nodded towards the door. 'Let's have a little team talk,' he suggested to Tom. 'Out in the corridor.'

So Tom followed the teacher, while the rest of the class held their noses and pretended to choke.

'OK. What's the story?' Leftie insisted, standing at a safe distance, with his arms folded, while Tom delivered his explanation.

'Dunno what you're on about...well...erm,

Mum was too busy to wash my stuff—
she's still got a hangover from Dad's
surprise do...and the hot water's off...
and I've been helping Nick mend his
bike...and fix the drains!'

'Nice try, but what's the real story?'
Leftie asked.

Tom sighed, then came out with it.
'I wanted to put Lola Kidman off
fancying me.'

Leftie smirked. 'Tom Bean, that's so
totally mad that I believe you!'

'S true.' Tom hung his head. 'And now
she's not even here!'

'Waste of time, huh?' Suggesting
that Tom run along to the shower block,
clean up, and change into his games kit
for the day, Leftie went smiling back into
the classroom.

'Bummer!' Tom stood under the hot shower,
running through all the bad words he knew.
'Bumming heck! Freaking Nora! Soggy-

stinking- beeping-
bummer!'

Tom hated school
showers. The water
hit your skin like
sharp needles and it
was never hot
enough. Then it
automatically cut
out when you were
still covered in soap.
You had to run out
into the changing room and flick the switch
on again, catching your death of cold.

Tom dashed in, out, then in again, like
a slippery eel. Once the soap was off, he
dived for a towel, flicked it over himself,
then jumped into his footie shirt, tracksuit
bottoms and trainers. Bundling his manky
uniform into his bag, he dumped it in his
locker and headed back to class.

'Ah, Tom, glad to see you scrub up so
well!' Leftie greeted him with a friendly

grin. 'Welcome to Geography. We're drawing a street map of the route between here and the Steelers' Highfield ground, if you'd like to join us.'

'Talking of Steelers,' Kingsley whispered to Tom as he sat down next to him. 'Guess where Lola is?'

'Don't know, don't care!' Tom hissed. As long as Miss Superglue wasn't here, he was happy.

'She's at Highfield!' Kingsley told him. 'Leftie had a message from the office. Lola's mum got her in with the TV crew. They've gone to interview the Steelers' new signing, Jesus Ardilo. It's true! On my life, dude, cross my heart and hope to die!'

Eight

'No way!'

'She's making it up!'

'I bet she's in bed with the flu!'

As the rumour flew round the class, through Assembly and out across the playground at morning break, few pupils at Woodbridge Junior were prepared to believe the story about Lola Kidman and Jesus Ardilo. It was like saying that Kingsley was world pro-skating champion, or that Jimmy Black had been signed for the England squad.

'I bet it's true!' By lunchtime, Bex Stevens was sick of the non-believers. 'Lola wouldn't make up a thing like that. You're all jealous, that's all!'

'Whoo-ooh!' Ryan and Kalid cried. 'Cool it, Bex. Don't get your knickers in a twist!'

'Anyway, we'll soon find out. Here comes Lola now!' Sasha yelled above the racket.

Tom stopped in his tracks.

'Pass the ball, Heinz!' Jimmy yelled.

But Tom had heard the jinx word, 'Lola'. 'I'm outta here!' he muttered, abandoning his football and vanishing behind the bike shed.

'Hey, Lola!' Danielle, Sasha and Bex sprang on her as soon as she came through the gate. 'You jammy thing! What's he like? C'mon, give us the goss!'

'Watch it. Let me breathe!' Lola emerged from the scrum of screaming girls.

'Girls, girls!' Miss Ambler strode across in her lace-up shoes and billowing skirt. She must have been the only person in the school not to have heard about Lola's invite to the Ardilo press conference. 'Whatever's the matter?'

'Nothing, it's OK!' Lola's face was glowing as she waved a bulging plastic carrier bag in the air. 'Guess what's in here.'

The crowd grew bigger and more out of control as Kingsley, Jimmy, Kalid, Ryan and Wayne joined the girls.

'Children!' Rambler Ambler bleated. But she was soon surrounded, and swallowed up.

'It's a football,' Bex guessed.

'Yeah, but not just any old football,' Lola told them. She jumped on to a low stone wall so that everyone could see. Then she drew the object out of the bag. 'This ball has been personally signed by every single Steelers first team player!'

'Wow! Cool! Mega! Wicked!' the crowd gasped. Even the non-believers had to believe.

It was no good. Tom couldn't resist. He stepped out of hiding for a closer look.

'Did Robbie Exley sign it?' Jimmy asked.

Lola pointed to the star striker's scribbled name.

Tom's eyes were on stalks. In the excitement, he forgot about keeping out

of Lola's way and pushed right through to
the front of the crowd.

'What about Ardilo?' Kingsley demanded.

'Here!' Lola pointed again.

'Did you meet him? What's he like?' the
girls chorused.

'He's cool. He doesn't speak much English
though. He's really really tanned.'

'Tell us what he said!' Danielle pleaded.

Lola sighed at the memory. 'They sat him
down in front of the camera, and he said,
"I am mucho-very 'appy to be 'ere at
'Ighfield. I 'ope the fans are 'appy also." '

'Wow, cool!' Boys and girls alike pictured
the amazing scene. 'Will it be on TV
tonight?'

Lola nodded. 'I watched him train with
the team for half an hour, then they came
off the pitch and Ardilo gave me this
signed photo.'

'Let's see!' The girls shrieked and tried to
grab the picture.

'That's enough!' Miss Ambler cried. 'The

bell's gone. I want everyone inside now!'

Grumbling, the crowd slowly broke up and shuffled off. All except Tom, who couldn't take his eyes off that magic ball.

'Hey, Tom!' Lola said airily, jumping down from the wall. 'How cool is this?'

He started to speak, then backed away.

'Yeah, cool,' he agreed. Lola had shoved the photo under his nose. It showed a footballer with long, jet-black hair held by a hairband (yeah, a hairband! Tom double-checked). His jaw was square, his nose broad and straight.

'Oh, Tom, I wish you'd been there,' Lola sighed, fluttering her eyelashes at him. 'It was gnarly!'

'Show me the ball again,' he muttered. He wanted to see if Kevin Crowe, the

Steelers' manager, had signed it, too.

'Careful with it,' Lola handed over the ball with both hands.

Just at that moment there was a bellow from the main entrance. 'Lola, I'd like a little word!'

Uh-oh. Waymann was on the warpath. She stood in the doorway, beckoning with her witchy fingernails, while all the other kids, including Kingsley and Kalid, slid past.

'Yeah, well, see ya!' Tom muttered, flinging Lola's precious ball back at her.

'Thomas Bean, that includes you!' Mrs Waymann shouted. 'Both of you, come to my office!'

And now Tom wished he'd stayed out of the way, behind the bike shed. An interview with Waymann was the last thing he needed, on top of the Superglue problem.

Reluctantly, he and Lola trotted into school. Past Danielle and Sasha.

'Ah, bless!' Sasha cooed. 'The doomed duo, the tragic twosome!'

'Shurrup, Sasha!' Tom and Lola snarled back.

Waymann's office always looked huge. The ceiling was high; there was a mile of patterned carpet and a desk the size of a snooker table. Waymann herself sat in a cloud of perfume, wearing bright red lipstick and pointed fingernails.

Tom gritted his teeth. *What had he done wrong this time?* he wondered. Was it not handing in his maths homework, or climbing the high wall at the back of the playground? Maybe talking in Assembly and blaming Wayne? It could be anything, so he squared his shoulders and waited for the blow to fall.

But first, Waymann turned to Lola with what seemed to be a smile.

'Lola, dear,' she began. The shiny cushion squeaked as she eased herself into her seat. 'Your mother telephoned about your absence from school, and I've been hearing

about your most exciting morning!'

'Yes, Mrs Waymann!' Lola's head was up, she looked proud and happy as she held her trophy ball in front of her.

'What a privilege for one of our pupils!' Waymann cooed, like a smug grey pigeon. 'Mrs Kidman tells me that you received a signed football. I'm sure it must make you the envy of every schoolchild in the country.'

'Yes, Mrs Waymann!' Tom scowled behind Lola's back. She was definitely overdoing the smarm.

'So, I've been wondering, dear, whether or not you would be so kind as to lend your football to Woodbridge Junior for a short period—so that we could put it into the glass showcase in the entrance hall.' Waymann's smile never flickered. 'I'm sure all our visitors would be fascinated to see it!'

Tom could tell that Lola was hesitating to let go of her prize possession, and he didn't blame her. But saying no to the head teacher was risky, like being in a cage with a tiger and turning your back. Those red claws, that toothy grin...

'Well, what do you say?' Waymann pressed Lola.

Lola nodded and slowly offered the ball.

'That's very generous of you, Lola dear.' The cushion squeaked as the headteacher leaned across the desk to take it. 'And before you go, I have a little word of advice.'

'Yes, Mrs Waymann.'

'I've called Tom in here because of his appearance.'

Tom glanced down at his footie shirt, tracksuit bottoms and trainers.

Waymann frowned. 'You see that he's not wearing a stitch of correct school uniform.'

'Please Mrs Waymann, Mr Wright told me—'

'Quiet!' Waymann cut in. 'I'm not interested in your feeble excuses, Tom. No doubt you were about to offer some totally ludicrous reason that I don't want to hear.'

Lucky! Tom thought. She'd never have believed him, anyway.

'No, Lola, I'm holding Thomas Bean up to you as an example NOT to follow!'

'Yes, Mrs Waymann.'

'I've been a little worried to see you, er... associating with Tom, lately,' the Head went on. 'My advice is, choose your friends carefully. After all, we don't want anyone leading you astray!' She raised her eyebrows and looked piercingly in Tom's direction.

'No, Mrs Waymann.'

Wow, thanks! Tom could hardly believe his ears. Was Waymann actually telling Lola not to hang around with him' Lucky, or what! Little did she know it, but Witchy-Woo Waymann had solved all his problems!

The head teacher tapped Lola's football with her forefinger. 'And, Tom, I want to see you here in my room, first thing tomorrow morning, correctly dressed in your school uniform!'

He stepped forward, grinning broadly. 'Yes, Mrs Waymann!' *Yes, yes, yes!*

'Of course, you say Yes, and you mean No,' Lola commented to Tom on their way back to the classroom.

Oh, rats! he thought. For a few moments he had tasted freedom.

'Yeah, I mean, just because Waymann says not to be friends with you, doesn't mean I can't be really!' Lola was walking slowly, clutching her signed photo of Ardilo instead of her precious football.

'Doesn't it?' Tom gasped, cast down into the depths of despair again. Down-up-down, like a yo-yo.

'No way!' she insisted,

stopping to face him and ignoring Fat Lennox's heavy tread down the corridor towards them. 'I'll always be your friend, Tom, for ever and ever!'

'You will?' Tom groaned. Stuck with Lola. Permanently.

'But,' she went on, 'from now on, I can't be your GIRLfriend.'

'Say that again!' he squeaked.

Plod-plod-plod-slurp-plod. Lennox advanced.

'I'm sorry, Tom. I really am. But I can't cheat on you. I have to tell you that I've gone and got another boyfriend!'

'Who?' he gasped. His head whirled. His world stood on its head. Freedom, here I come!

Lola smoothed the photo in her hand and showed it to Tom.

'Ardilo,' she whispered, pressing the picture against her chest. 'It's no good, Tom. It was love at first sight!'

Tom punched the air. His ex-girlfriend

had fallen in love with a man who wore a hairband! Tom jumped and twirled, fell down on his knees, and hugged the caretaker's dog.

Huff-huff-slurp! Lennox rolled over with shock.

'Cut it out!' Bernie King appeared round the corner. 'Lennox, get up and stop making a show of yourself. You don't know where that boy's been!'

'La-la-la-lah!' Tom sang as he threw his dirty uniform into the washing machine and popped his head through the neck-hole of a clean T-shirt. 'Da-da-diddley-dee!'

'Someone's happy,' Beth commented.

'See ya, Mum! See ya, Dad!' Tom was off to the park, board in hand, shades perched on the end of his nose. Slamming down his board, he popped a moving nollie combined with a heelflick. Wicked!

'Hey, Tom, where's Lola?' Snidey Danielle called from the street corner.

'Highfield!' he yelled back as he whizzed by. 'She's hanging around the players' gate, waiting for Ardilo to come out!'

'So where are you off to, then?' Danielle wanted to know.

'The park, with the crew!' He pulled a grind along the kerb then shot between two posts.

King of the deck, no worries!

Tell the Me Truth, Tom!

Jenny Oldfield

Tom eyeballs a fox in Bernie King's basement, but no one believes him. 'No way! Dream on, Tom!' say his friends. Tom decides to prove it. He's going to take a picture of the fox...After all, the camera never lies...Does it?

Watch Out, Wayne

Jenny Oldfield

Life's tough for Tom. He offers to be best mates with new boy Wayne, but it only lands him in trouble—again! OK, maybe giving Wayne a CRASH course in skateboarding wasn't so smart.
But Tom meant well. Honest!

Keep the Noise Down, Kingsley

Jenny Oldfield

Tom has a rival at school. Kingsley is a mega annoying show-off! He's lary, he's brash, and he's really getting on everyone's nerves! Tom needs to find a way to break it to Kingsley that he's got to pipe down! But how?

Drop Dead, Danielle

Jenny Oldfield

Mean and mardy 'dob-them-in' Danielle is on Tom's case again-accusing him of flooding the school cloakroom! *As if.* Danielle says she's going to tell on Tom—and she probably will! Tom needs to prove it wasn't him—but how?

Don't Make Me Laugh, Liam

Jenny Oldfield

Tom's cousin Liam is coming over from
Dublin. Wicked! Liam is just like Tom–only ten
times noisier, and even more of a joker–he'll
probably give Tom a few handy tips! Uh-oh.
As if he really needs any encouragement...